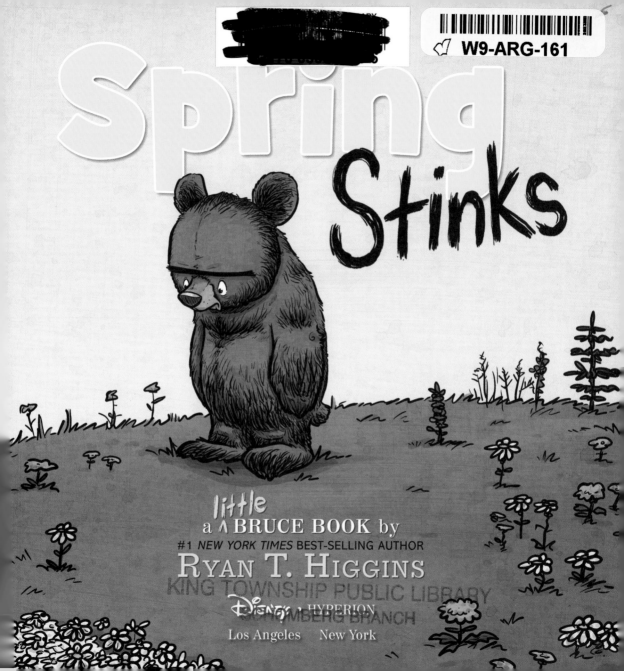

Spring Stinks

a *little* ∧ **BRUCE BOOK** by
#1 *NEW YORK TIMES* BEST-SELLING AUTHOR

RYAN T. HIGGINS

Disney • HYPERION
Los Angeles   New York

It is springtime
in Soggy Hollow,

and everyone is happy.

Everyone
but Bruce.

"I love the smells of spring!" says Ruth.

"Spring stinks," says Bruce.

Ruth has a basket.
A very nice basket.
"Let's smell some smelly springtime
smells together," says Ruth.

"That is
my basket,"
says Bruce.

"Ooooh . . . the green smell
of green-smelling grass!" says Ruth.

"Grrrr!" grumbles Bruce.

"Aaaah . . . the sweet smell of sweet-smelling daisies," says Ruth.

"Rrrr!" rumbles Bruce.

"Mmmm . . . the woodsy smell of woodsy-smelling trees," says Ruth.

"Ouch," mumbles Bruce.

"Ooh-ooh-ooh! You're going to LOVE the next one!" says Ruth.

"Wet moose!"

"Get out of
my basket."

Bruce does not like
the smell of wet moose.

"I know!" says Ruth.
"Bears love the smell of honey!"

Uh-oh.

This smells like trouble.

BEEEEEEELINE

"Spring stinks," says Bruce.

"It sure does!" says Ruth.